Silver Dolphins

RISING STAR

D1491219

For Greta and for Stewart – my twin.

First published in paperback by HarperCollins *Children's Books* in 2010

HarperCollins *Children's Books* is a division of HarperCollins*Publishers* Ltd,
77-85 Fulham Palace Road, Hammersmith, London W6 8JB.

Visit our website at: www.harpercollins.co.uk

1 3 5 7 9 10 8 6 4 2
ISBN-13: 978-0-00-734812-1

Text copyright © Julie Sykes 2010
Cover illustrations copyright © Andrew Farley 2010

The author and illustrator assert the moral right to be identified
as the author and illustrator of the work.

A CIP catalogue record for this title is available from the British Library.
All rights reserved.

Typeset by Palimpsest Book Production Limited, Grangemouth, Stirlingshire

Conditions of Sale
This book is sold subject to the condition that it shall not, by way of trade
or otherwise, be lent, re-sold, hired out or otherwise circulated without
the publisher's prior written consent in any form of binding or cover other
than that in which it is published and without a similar condition including
this condition being imposed on the subsequent purchaser.

Mixed Sources
Product group from well-managed
forests and other controlled sources
www.fsc.org Cert no. SW-COC-1806
© 1996 Forest Stewardship Council
FSC

FSC is a non-profit international organisation established to promote the
responsible management of the world's forests. Products carrying the FSC
label are independently certified to assure consumers that they come
from forests that are managed to meet the social, economic and
ecological needs of present and future generations.

Find out more about HarperCollins and the environment at
www.harpercollins.co.uk/green

by Summer Waters

Silver Dolphins

RISING STAR

HarperCollins *Children's Books*

Prologue

A long way out at sea, a small dolphin with a cheeky smile was swimming by himself when a sharp whistle startled him. Suddenly alert, Bubbles listened to the cry for help.

"Mum! Where are you?"

Bubbles knew that voice! At once he changed direction and swam towards the dolphin in distress.

"Dot!" he clicked. "What are you doing so far out at sea on your own?"

Dot was younger than Bubbles and much smaller than him.

"Bubbles!" she squeaked, delighted to see

a familiar face. "Mum said I could go off and play… but I got lost."

"Home's this way," clicked Bubbles kindly. "Follow me."

Bubbles kept checking that Dot was behind him as he led the little dolphin back to their pod.

"Mum!" squeaked Dot, suddenly spotting her mother. "Thanks, Bubbles." She rubbed her nose against his shyly and swam to join her mum.

Bubbles continued on until he found his own family. Spirit, Star and Dream were swimming together near the kelp beds.

"Dad, you'll never guess what?" clicked Bubbles. "Dot's mum let her play on her own and she got lost. Luckily I found her."

Spirit patted Bubbles with a fin.

"Well done, son," he clicked.

"How could Dot's mum let her go off like that?" asked Bubbles. "Wasn't it dangerous?"

Spirit rolled over thoughtfully, his silver skin sparkling in the sunlit water.

"It's hard letting children go off and do things on their own, but you have to, or they'll never learn," he said eventually.

Bubbles stayed quiet for a moment, then smiled in understanding.

"Like the Silver Dolphins. They learnt by doing things on their own."

Spirit nodded.

"Just like the Silver Dolphins continue to."

"But I thought the Silver Dolphins knew everything they needed to know now," said Bubbles.

"There is always more to learn," said Spirit wisely.

"But you know everything, don't you, Dad?" Bubbles persisted.

Spirit clicked a laugh.

"I wish I did," he sighed. "But even I have more to learn."

Chapter One

"I won!" Antonia Lee burst through the surface of the water, her arms triumphantly stretched above her head.

"Well done, Flipper Feet," clicked Bubbles, "but you only won because I gave you a head start."

"No you didn't," laughed Antonia.

"Did," clicked Bubbles, playfully splashing her with water.

"Water fight," shouted Cai, surfacing with Dream. "Girls against boys."

"You're on," clicked everyone.

Dream swam over to Antonia, Cai joined Bubbles and soon the sea was foaming like a shaken bottle of shampoo as they splashed each other with water.

"Truce!" panted Antonia at last.

Treading water, she pushed her long blonde hair out of her eyes.

"That was such fun!" clicked Bubbles happily. "I'm glad you're back. We missed you loads, didn't we, Dream?"

Dream nodded fervently and clicked, "It wasn't the same without you."

"We missed you too," said Antonia.

She and Cai had just returned from a trip to Australia to visit Cai's parents, who worked over there. Cai was temporarily living in Sandy Bay with his Aunty Claudia, who ran a marine conservation charity called Sea Watch.

"Let's have another race," said Bubbles.

Antonia shook her head. "Sorry, Bubbles, but there isn't time. We've swam much further than we normally do and I promised Mum I'd be home early. School starts again tomorrow and I've got to get my things ready."

"Don't go to school," said Bubbles. "Come and swim with us instead. We can show you lots of new things."

"I bet you can," said Antonia. "But we still have to go to school."

"I'll go and get the rubbish," said Cai. He turned and swam towards a small beach nestling at the foot of the cliffs.

"Wait for me." Antonia swam quickly after him.

Antonia and Cai had been litter picking. It was part of their role as Silver Dolphins to protect the seas and all the creatures living there. Whenever the Silver Dolphins were needed, Spirit called to them through the silver dolphin charms that Antonia and Cai always wore. A very special magic let them swim and communicate with their dolphin friends. Today Spirit had called them to clear some floating rubbish he'd found.

When it was shallow enough Antonia and Cai stood on the seabed and waded up the beach.

"It's a shame there's no bin on the beach. We'll have to be careful how we get this back," said Cai, picking up the strips of polystyrene packaging they'd found. "This stuff is lethal if an animal eats it."

"I know," said Antonia gravely. "It breaks up into tiny balls that don't rot and are left in the sea forever."

They shared the polystyrene between them, being careful not to snap it.

"Where are we?" Antonia wondered aloud. She looked up at the cliffs. "There's a lot of noise coming from up there."

"I think this is Crane Point," Cai answered. "Aunty Claudia told me there's a block of luxury apartments being built on the cliff top here. There was a story about it in the Sandy

Bay newspaper. Lots of people don't want the apartments to be built because they'll spoil the view and bring more traffic to the area. Most of the apartments are being sold as holiday lets."

"I don't blame them," said Antonia hotly. "It's lovely here."

"Aunty Claudia says it's not all bad," said Cai. "The building project has created lots of jobs and the tourists will too when they start visiting."

"True." Antonia walked backwards down the beach, keeping her eyes on the top of the cliffs for signs of building activity. "But the builders should be more responsible. This looks like their rubbish. They should clear up properly and not dump things in the sea."

"Maybe it blew away," said Cai reasonably.

"That's not clearing up properly," Antonia argued, hoping this wasn't going to be the start of a bigger problem.

They swam back to Bubbles and his mum Star, who looked at the polystyrene inquisitively.

"It seems harmless," clicked Bubbles, "but Dad says it can kill us."

His sister Dream shivered. "Thanks for taking it away," she clicked.

Bubbles and Dream swam with the Silver Dolphins back to Claudia's beach.

"Goodbye," clicked Bubbles. "And if you change your mind about going to school we can teach you lots of new things."

Antonia and Cai laughed.

"See you soon." Antonia rubbed noses with Bubbles and then Dream.

As the dolphins swam back out to sea Antonia trod water for a moment, reluctant to go home. She'd had a brilliant summer and wasn't keen to go to school the following day.

"That's it then, the summer's over," sighed Cai, echoing her gloomy thoughts.

"It doesn't feel like it," said Antonia, slowly swimming towards the shore. "It's still really hot. I don't want to sit in a stuffy old classroom all day."

"Me neither," agreed Cai. "Especially now we're in Year Six. Mrs Howard said she's going to work us extra hard."

They waded up the beach. The Silver Dolphin magic made the sea water pour off

them like a mini waterfall until their clothes were completely dry. Antonia shook out her damp hair and Cai pulled a face as he ran his fingers through his.

"The water makes my hair go extra curly," he laughed.

They sat on the warm sand to put on their sandals, then went through the gate that led to Claudia's garden.

Claudia was talking to a builder who was making a deepwater pool for injured sea animals. She waved and called out, "Are you staying to tea, Antonia?"

"Not tonight, thanks," said Antonia. "I promised I'd be home early."

"See you tomorrow then," said Cai after they'd put their rubbish in the Sea Watch bin.

"See you," said Antonia.

On the way home Antonia stopped halfway up Sandy Bay Road to look at the sea. A funny feeling was bothering her, and her thoughts strayed to the building site at Crane Point. Staring at the bright blue water, Antonia strongly sensed that Mrs Howard wasn't the only one who would be keeping them busy that term.

Chapter Two

ntonia!" Sophie was waiting at the end of her drive, but when she saw Antonia she ran to meet her. They hugged until they almost toppled over.

"When did you get back from Australia? Did you have a good time?" Sophie bombarded Antonia with questions as they walked to school.

"I got you a present," said Antonia, when she could get a word in edgeways. "I'll give it to you when we get to school. Do you think Mrs Howard will let us sit together?"

"I doubt it," Sophie giggled. "I expect Miss Brown has told her that we chat too much."

In the school playground Antonia swung her bag to the ground and rummaged inside for the miniature wooden boomerang she'd bought for Sophie. As she handed it over Lauren Hampton barged past. Antonia dropped the neatly wrapped present, but luckily Sophie caught it.

"Watch it!" cried Sophie hotly.

"Watch what?" asked Lauren nastily. "It's not my fault that Antonia got in my way."

Sophie went red with indignation, but Antonia steered her to another part of the playground before she could protest.

"Ignore her," she said. "She's not worth it."

"Ooh!" exclaimed Sophie crossly. "I don't know why she's always so nasty to you. Thanks for the boomerang, Antonia. It's lovely. I'll ask Dad to help me hang it on my bedroom wall."

Cai and Toby arrived as the bell went and they all walked into school.

"Let's sit together," said Cai, but Mrs Howard had other ideas.

"Just my luck," groaned Antonia when her new teacher called out, "Charlie West, Lauren Hampton, Antonia Lee and Harry Lucas on this table, please."

Antonia hurried to her new place, hoping to sit next to one of the boys, but Charlie and Harry beat her there and she was forced to sit next to Lauren.

"Move up, Toni," said Lauren, making herself as wide as possible when she sat down.

"It's 'Antonia'. I might not know you're talking to me if you call me Toni."

"Good. Then I won't have to talk to you, Toni," said Lauren unkindly.

It was one of the longest days Antonia had ever spent in school. The work was much harder than it had been in Year Five and Antonia's brain felt rusty after the long summer holiday. Lauren had a brand new pencil case and a bumper pack of gel pens that she laid out, taking up more than her fair

share of the desk and she grumbled each time Antonia accidentally touched one.

"My dad got me those," she boasted. "He's got this great new job over at Crane Point. It's my birthday next week and Dad said I can have a huge party. I'm going to invite everyone in the class." Lauren paused and her eyes narrowed to mean slits. "Well, almost everyone," she added.

At the end of the day Antonia's table was the last to be let out as Lauren wouldn't stop talking. When they were free to go Antonia rushed to the cloakroom to get her bag.

"Slow coach," teased Cai. "Don't you want to go home?"

"I'm not going home. I'm going to Sea Watch with you."

"That *is* home!" said Cai.

Antonia grinned. Sea Watch was like a second home for her, and Claudia treated Antonia like she was part of the family. Shortly after arriving at Sea Watch they were joined by Emily, Karen and Eleanor, straight from their first day at their new secondary school. Antonia felt a little shy when the girls first came in. They looked so grown up in their new green school uniform. But underneath they were still the same, chattering excitedly about their day as they all went outside to see how the deepwater pool was coming along.

"Not you lot again," teased the builder good-naturedly. "I'd be finished much more quickly if you stopped checking up on me."

"Let's go and see what Claudia wants us to do today," said Antonia.

Claudia had an important job for them: cleaning out Tilly the seal's pen and feeding her. Tilly had been in a very bad way when she first arrived at Sea Watch, but under Claudia's watchful eye she'd regained her health and was slowly putting on weight.

Antonia and Cai wore plastic gloves and aprons to clean out the pen. They scrubbed out Tilly's water bowl and refilled it with fresh water, then swept and hosed down the enclosure. Tilly watched them with big eyes, her whiskery nose inquisitively nudging the cleaning equipment.

"She's like a puppy," laughed Cai, when Tilly tried to follow them back to the Sea Watch building.

Tilly grew very excited when Antonia and Cai returned with a bucket of fish. Grunting loudly, she almost butted the bucket from their hands. She was wolfing down her last fish when a familiar sensation swept over Antonia. Spirit was about to call. Seconds later the silver dolphin charm hanging round her neck vibrated.

Silver Dolphin, the charm called to her. *We need your help.*

Spirit, I hear your call, Antonia called back silently.

When Antonia first became a Silver Dolphin she'd always cover the charm with her hand even though she knew only a Silver Dolphin could see it move and hear its shrill whistling.

She glanced over to Cai to check he was

following and together they ran down the garden, hurdling the low gate that opened on to the beach.

"New shoes are a pain," grunted Cai, as he struggled to get his off.

"Sandals are much easier," agreed Antonia, throwing her shoes and socks into the Sea Watch boat with Cai's.

They raced across the powder-soft sand and splashed into the sea. Antonia dived into the water, loving the moment her legs melded together to work like a dolphin's tail.

Sensing the call was urgent, Antonia propelled herself through the water even faster than a real dolphin as she headed towards Spirit.

"We're being called in the same direction as yesterday," panted Cai.

Suddenly Antonia had a bad feeling about this call. She dived in and out of the waves, her tail-like legs powering her along until she saw a magnificent silver head bobbing in the water close to the shore.

"Silver Dolphins." Spirit was relieved to see them. "This is an emergency. There's a puffin colony at the top of the cliffs. It's not safe any more because of a new building site close by. The puffins are in danger of being run over on the road to the building site. Please help them."

Antonia's heart sank. This was another serious threat to local wildlife. Annoyed that she hadn't thought to investigate further yesterday, she screwed up her eyes and stared at the cliffs. It was impossible to tell that there were puffins up there from here. Spirit must

have used his special Silver Dolphin powers to know about them and their problem. To the left Antonia noticed a narrow path winding upwards. It was long and very steep. Would there be time to save the puffins?

"Hurry," urged Spirit.

Antonia pulled herself together. She and Cai were Silver Dolphins. They could do this! She struck out for the shore, emerging from the water and hurtling across the beach with Cai.

"The path's this way," she cried.

Antonia and Cai veered left, hopped up a short flight of steps and started the steep climb to the top of the cliff.

Chapter Three

The narrow cliff path was bordered with long grass that tickled Antonia's legs and prickly brambles that snatched at her clothes, but luckily the Silver Dolphin magic protected her bare feet as she ran. Halfway to the top her lungs began to burn and after a while she had to stop to catch her breath. Cai stopped too, bending his

body forward and resting his hands on his knees as he greedily gulped air. There wasn't time to hang around for long. They took off quickly again, half running half jogging, until finally they burst on to the cliff top, scattering the resident puffins, who mewled like startled cats.

"Sorry," called Antonia softly.

Carefully she moved among the adult birds, marvelling at how many of them there were.

"Look, Cai, baby puffins! Aren't they sweet?"

"Quick," shouted Cai. "They're heading for the road."

On surprisingly nimble legs a group of baby pufflings began waddling straight for the brand-new road that sliced the cliff top in two. It looked very out of place in such a beautiful spot, as did the building site it lead to. Amid heavy

machinery and scaffolding the workers were packing up for the day. Antonia and Cai ran after the pufflings, overtaking them and waving their arms to shoo them back to their nests. In the building-site car park doors slammed and engines revved as everyone headed home.

"Watch out, Antonia!" warned Cai. "Keep off the road while the cars are leaving the site."

"You too," said Antonia, who was already keeping a careful eye on the traffic.

The pufflings were a slippery bunch. Each time Antonia and Cai managed to herd them back to the safety of the cliff top, a small but determined group would suddenly dash back the opposite way. Most of the workmen were very careful, slowing their cars when they saw Antonia and Cai by the side of the road. But

not everyone slowed down. Suddenly a battered red car drew up alongside them. For a wild moment Antonia thought the driver was going to offer to help, but she couldn't have been more wrong.

"Nutty kids!" The driver, a thickset man with small eyes, hung out of the side window laughing unpleasantly. "Aint got nothing better to do than play with the birdies? Where are your shoes, losers?"

Music blared from his open car window, startling the pufflings and making them run in confused circles. Laughing raucously, the driver revved up his engine and drove away.

"What an idiot!" exclaimed Cai, his face red with anger.

"Forget him," soothed Antonia. She hopped

sideways to prevent a breakaway group of pufflings from slipping past her.

It was a full fifteen minutes before the last car left the building site, but by that time Antonia and Cai had somehow persuaded the pufflings to explore the area along the cliffs instead of the roadside.

"It's beautiful," said Antonia, shielding her eyes from the late afternoon sun.

There were puffins everywhere. The black and white adult birds with their clown-like eyes, brightly coloured beaks and distinctive orange legs were so pretty. So was the craggy cliff top, whose muted greys and greens contrasted sharply with the colourful birds.

"I love the way the puffins sit in rocky hollows so you can only see their heads

peeping out," said Cai. "They look like they're watching us."

"I don't blame them," said Antonia, laughing. "Not all people are friendly. I love the pufflings. They're so adorable I want to pick them up and cuddle them."

"That's nature's way of protecting them," said Cai, his voice becoming serious. "Baby animals are usually cute so you feel you have to look after them."

Slowly, keeping well away from the cliff edge, they walked among the birds, stopping now and then for a closer look. Even though Antonia would have loved to cuddle the baby pufflings, she knew she mustn't. Wild animals weren't pets. It wasn't safe for them to become too friendly with humans, and some animals

could inflict nasty wounds by pecking, scratching or biting, if they were frightened.

"I think we're done here now," said Antonia, once they'd walked around the whole colony. Her eyes swept the road, totally empty of traffic now the builders had packed up and gone home.

"For today," said Cai.

"Yes," said Antonia, immediately catching his meaning. She looked over to the building site, her grey-green eyes troubled. "So how do we stop the same thing happening tomorrow afternoon?"

"And in the morning. Now the pufflings are ready to leave their nests they'll want to keep on exploring. They'll be in danger first thing in the morning when the workmen arrive for work too," mused Cai.

"You're right," said Antonia thoughtfully, as they headed down the cliff path in single file. She was silent as she concentrated on walking down the narrow cliff path. But as she jumped down the last step and on to the beach she smiled triumphantly.

"I've got it. We need a puffling patrol."

"Pardon?" said Cai.

"Puffling patrol," Antonia repeated excitedly. "You know, like the schools that have a lollipop person to help children cross the road. We could do something similar for the puffins. We could do a puffling patrol at the beginning and end of the day to keep the pufflings *away* from the road."

"That's a brilliant idea," said Cai, his brown eyes shining excitedly.

"It would mean getting up really early," warned Antonia.

"I know, Claudia's builder starts at the crack of dawn!" said Cai. "It's going to take up all our spare time," he added, "although Claudia will help. I bet she'll drive us and take us back again so we're not late for school."

They padded across the beach and waded into the water.

"Where's Spirit?" asked Cai suddenly. "He usually waits for us."

"Over there, near the rocks. There's someone with him." Antonia's heart leapt. "I hope it's Bubbles or Dream. I'd love a game of sprat."

"It's too big for either of them," said Cai, gazing into the distance. "It's Star."

"Oh!" Antonia tried not to be disappointed. She loved Star too but, like her own mum, Star was always too busy to play.

"It's probably a good thing it's not Bubbles and Dream," said Cai sensibly. "We need to get back and ask Claudia if she'll help with the puffins."

"Yes!" sighed Antonia. "And I better not be too late home, especially if I'm going to get Mum to agree to me going out so early tomorrow."

Mrs Lee was very strict about knowing where Antonia was and what time she'd be back. She knew nothing about the Silver Dolphins as Antonia had to keep the magic a secret. Claudia, who was a Silver Dolphin and knew when Antonia and Cai were answering a call, didn't worry so much.

Cai was about to launch himself into the sea, but he paused. "Your mum will let you go tomorrow, won't she?" he asked.

Antonia said nothing for a moment, enjoying the magical feeling of being in the sea and knowing that soon she would be diving through the waves as fast as a dolphin.

"Yes," she said slowly, sounding more certain than she felt.

But what if Mum wouldn't let her go? Antonia cast the thought aside. She would worry about that if it happened. Plunging headfirst into the water she swam to join Spirit and Star, joyfully leaping in and out of the waves, glittering drops of sea spray flying from her body like diamonds.

Chapter Four

"I don't know, Antonia," said Mum, when Antonia asked if she could go with Cai to do an early-morning puffling patrol at the building site. "It sounds dangerous. And what about school? Year Six is an important year."

"Please, Mum," Antonia wheedled. "I'll be really careful, and I promise I won't be late for school."

"I think she should go," said Dad. "Claudia's very responsible. She wouldn't let her Sea Watch helpers do anything dangerous. It's good for young people to get involved with the environment. After all, it's their future."

Antonia went quiet. It was true – Claudia wouldn't allow them to do anything dangerous on purpose – but being a Silver Dolphin was full of risks.

"All right, you can go. Wear something bright so you can be easily seen, and no running around in the road! Stay on the path. And don't be late for school or I will ground you for the whole term!" said Mum sternly.

"Thanks Mum, thanks Dad!" Antonia hugged her parents.

She phoned Sophie first, to tell her not to

wait for her the following morning. Then she phoned Cai to give him the good news.

That night, to be on the safe side, Antonia borrowed an alarm clock from her little sister Jessica and set it five minutes after her own was due to go off. She needn't have worried. She woke before either of the alarms and leapt out of bed to open the blind covering her sloping attic window. The sky was a clear blue, but as Antonia stared through the open window she noticed small beads of condensation on the wooden frame. There was a slight nip to the early-morning air. She shivered, knowing sadly that summer would soon be over. Antonia brushed the tangles from her long blonde hair, dressed in her brightest clothes then packed her yellow and blue uniform in her school bag. After

a quick wash she crept downstairs and poured herself a bowl of cereal and a glass of milk. After stacking the dirty dishes in the dishwasher she pulled on her shoes before hurrying outside to wait for Cai and Claudia. Minutes later their car pulled on to the drive.

"Hi there," said Cai, twisting round in the front seat as Antonia climbed in the back.

The building site was deserted. Claudia turned the car round in the temporary car park. Her mobile phone rang as she turned the engine off, making everyone jump. Cai and Antonia got out of the car and Claudia waved and mouthed at them not to go too far.

"Sorry," she said, when she was able to join them. "There's a problem back at Sea Watch.

The builder needs a decision on something. Will you be all right if I leave you here? I'll be back in time to get you to school."

"Good," said Antonia. "Because Mum will ground me forever if I'm late."

"Quite right too," said Claudia. "Now I want you to promise me you'll both be careful. No running on to the road and stay away from the cliff edge too."

"Promise," said Antonia and Cai together.

"I'll come back up and have a proper look at the puffins later. I never realised there was a colony here. I'm surprised the builders got planning permission when the build was this close to their breeding ground," called Claudia, hurrying away.

For a brief moment as the car disappeared,

Antonia felt uneasy. The building site was enclosed by a high temporary metal fence standing in concrete blocks. She peered through the rectangular-shaped mesh at the silent concrete mixers, diggers and fork lifts. The machines stared defiantly back, as if they were waiting for her to turn away so they could leap to life and chase after her.

Are you all right? Do you want me to come back?

Embarrassed that Claudia had heard her thoughts, Antonia blushed so deeply that even her scalp turned pink.

No thanks. I'm fine, she answered silently.

Well done, Silver Dolphin!

"Antonia? I asked if you were ready." Cai tapped Antonia's arm.

"Sorry. I was miles away."

Cai gave her a knowing look. "I thought you were."

They headed towards the cliffs on the opposite side of the road to the new flats. It was too early for most of the adult puffins, who were hunkered down between the rocks. A few of the pufflings were beginning to stir, and it wasn't long before the more adventurous ones came out to explore. Antonia and Cai shepherded them back. It felt a much easier task than the day before, even when the builders started to arrive in their cars.

"We're getting good at this," said Cai, cheerfully directing a fluffy puffling in the opposite direction.

"Whoops! Spoke too soon," said Antonia,

as another cheeky puffling darted round Cai. "Go back to your friends, go on. Shoo!"

Purring indignantly the puffling shuffled away. Eventually the number of cars coming along the road slowed to a trickle and stopped. Antonia glared over at the building site, now in full swing.

"The poor puffins! It's so noisy," she complained.

"It won't be like this forever," said Cai. "Once the builders have gone things should quieten down."

"Then they'll be stuck with the flats. The people who don't want them built here are right. It spoils the view."

"I know," said Cai glumly. "But people have to live somewhere."

Antonia and Cai perched on a rock while they waited for Claudia.

"I don't want to go to school. I want to stay and keep an eye on the pufflings," said Antonia. "There might be more traffic during the day."

"School doesn't feel as important as the puffling's safety," Cai agreed.

"I can't believe Mrs Howard put me with Lauren." The thought had been niggling Antonia since yesterday.

"She's not bullying you, is she?" asked Cai sharply.

"It's nothing that I can't handle," said Antonia, not wanting a fuss.

"If it gets out of hand you'll tell someone?"

"I won't let it get out of hand," said Antonia lightly.

Antonia had hoped that by not reacting to Lauren the bigger girl would grow bored of annoying her. But at school Lauren continued to be a pain. She was crafty not to do anything too nasty, but the low-level incidents were getting Antonia down.

"Please stop prodding me with that ruler," said Antonia loudly, when Lauren dug her in the ribs for the third time.

Mrs Howard looked over, but Lauren had dropped the ruler and was studiously looking at her maths book. When Mrs Howard looked away Lauren whispered to Charlie and Harry.

"Are you coming to my party? It's gonna be great. Dad's hired a hall, we're having a disco inside and an inflatable slide outside. Mum's

getting caterers to do the food cos I'm inviting too many people for her to do it all."

"Cool. Are we invited then?" asked Harry.

"I'm inviting the whole class. Well, almost the whole class." Lauren paused and stared at Antonia. "I'm giving out the invitations tomorrow."

Antonia kept her head bent over her work and pretended she hadn't heard. She didn't want to go to Lauren's party, but she didn't want to be the only one in the class not invited. That would be horrible!

"How come you're having such a big party?" asked Charlie.

"Dad's got a new job. It's on a building site over at Crane Point. Hey, get this! Yesterday when he was leaving work he saw two kids playing with the gulls. They were running about waving their arms like they were trying to fly or something. Dad said it was hilarious."

"They weren't gulls, they were baby puffins," said Antonia. "And we were stopping them from getting run over."

Lauren stared at Antonia in gleeful amazement.

"It was you!" she exclaimed. "You were bird girl! How sad! You should have seen it. Dad did a wicked impression last night."

Lauren put her hands on her hips and stuck out her elbows, flapping her arms and making Charlie and Harry roll around the desk with laughter.

"Bird girl," they cackled. "Go on, Antonia, teach Lauren how to fly."

"Antonia's table," called Mrs Howard sharply. "There is far too much noise over there. Settle down or I will keep you in at break."

Smirking at Charlie and Harry Lauren picked up her pencil and pretended to work. Antonia was so furious she had to bite her lip from saying something rude. It wasn't fair. Couldn't her new teacher see she wasn't the one causing the trouble? Tightly gripping her own pencil Antonia forced herself to concentrate on her sums. But the Year Six work was hard and Antonia's thoughts kept straying to the pufflings. Would they be safe while she and Cai were at school?

Chapter Five

Sea Watch was just the thing to cheer Antonia up after a bad day at school. The deepwater pool was coming along nicely and the builder thought that Tilly the seal would be able to use it the following week.

"Tilly will love that," said Antonia.

The seal pup had been recovering at Sea

Watch for nearly a month and Antonia was convinced she missed being in the water.

"Claudia's asked if we could clean out her pen again," said Cai, "but I think we should ask someone else to do it so we can get back to Crane Point."

"Definitely," agreed Antonia. "I've been worrying about the pufflings all day."

They asked Emily to look after Tilly and she readily agreed. Claudia said she would run them to Crane Point in the car.

"There you go. Your first rescue," said Claudia, stopping the car in the middle of the road leading to the building site.

Antonia and Cai leapt out and shooed the puffling brazenly waddling towards them back towards the cliffs.

"Good luck," called Claudia through her open window. "I'd stay with you if it wasn't so busy at Sea Watch right now. I'll pick you up later." Slowly she turned the car around and drove away.

The pufflings kept Antonia and Cai busy until the workmen had left for the day and the building site was still and deserted. Cai plonked himself down on the rock they'd sat on that morning to wait for Claudia. Antonia hovered beside him, not wanting to get comfortable, as she had a strong feeling that their work wasn't over. The sensation grew until suddenly the silver dolphin charm around Antonia's neck twitched.

Spirit, I hear your call.

She glanced at Cai, smiling as the silver

dolphin badge pinned to his shirt also began to twitch. Suddenly both dolphin charms let out a loud whistle. Startled, Cai leapt to his feet.

"Spirit!" he exclaimed.

Antonia was already sprinting for the cliff path. Cai pounded after her shouting, "Spirit, I hear your call."

They thundered down the path as fast as they dared, their feet kicking up stones and sending them spinning ahead of them. Antonia's face was red and she was panting as she jumped from the end of the path, down the steps and on to the beach.

"Oomph!" exclaimed Cai, almost landing on top of her.

The call was urgent. Antonia sensed it even

without feeling her silver dolphin charm wildly thrashing against her neck. Pulling off her shoes and socks, she tossed them in the sand and raced down to the sea. Cai ran alongside her and together they splashed into the water, deeper and deeper until at last Antonia's legs began melding together. Relieved, she dived into the waves, her body arching and leaping in and out of the sea as she raced to answer Spirit's call. Graceful as real dolphins, and twice as fast, Antonia and Cai sped on.

"There," called Cai, suddenly spotting Spirit's silver head in the water.

Spirit was swimming in agitated circles, but stopped as the Silver Dolphins grew closer.

"Thank goodness you're here," he clicked. "A puffin is drowning out at sea."

Spirit led the way until Antonia and Cai saw a frightened bird struggling in the water.

"Steady," soothed Antonia, swimming closer.

Reaching the puffin, she stretched out and held on to its writhing body to keep its head above the water while she found out what was dragging the bird under. Its legs and body were tangled in a long sheet of plastic and the bird's efforts to free itself were making things worse.

"Hold him steady," said Cai, frantically tearing at the plastic with his bare hands.

The plastic was tough and wouldn't give, but eventually Cai made a small hole with his finger.

"Can I have a go? I might be able to..." Antonia trailed away, not wanting to sound

as if she was boasting, but thinking that maybe she could use her extra-special Silver Dolphin powers to free the bird.

"Yes please. Here, I'll hold the bird," said Cai readily.

Antonia passed the puffin to Cai, grateful that he never seemed fazed that she could do more than him. Carefully she wriggled her finger through the hole he'd made.

Rip, plastic, she thought, willing the plastic to tear open.

A warm sensation spread from her arms to her hand then down into her fingers. She flexed them gently, loving the tingling feeling of the magic.

Rip, plastic, thought Antonia, concentrating her thoughts.

She continued to hold her fingers against the plastic, wriggling the one that was poking through the hole. To her delight the plastic began to pop and dissolve in the same way candyfloss melts in your mouth.

"Steady," soothed Cai as the frightened puffin struggled harder.

The bird fixed Cai with a clownish eye then gradually relaxed, allowing Antonia to pull the sheet of plastic away. The legs were the most difficult part. Somehow the bird was completely trussed up and it took more of Antonia's special magic to melt the plastic. As the last piece of wrapping fell away Antonia moved back, expecting the puffin to fly out to sea. Instead it sat in the water, calmly fluffing up its feathers, watching the Silver Dolphins as

it gently bobbed up and down with the swell.

"Puffins are so pretty," said Antonia, admiring the bird's black and white face and brightly coloured beak.

"Aunty Claudia told me they spend most of their lives at sea," said Cai, swimming a short distance from the bird. "They only come ashore in the spring and summer to breed."

"You'd have thought they'd have safer lives spending it mostly at sea. But the sea is so polluted there's danger everywhere," reflected Antonia. Treading water, she held up the sheet of plastic.

"This packaging must have come from the building site."

Cai squinted at it, trying to make sense of the torn black lettering.

"I think it says 'plasterboard'. It definitely looks like builders' waste."

"Well done, Silver Dolphins." Spirit swam forward and thanked Antonia and Cai by rubbing his nose against theirs. "As always you did a good job."

Feeling embarrassed, Antonia coloured. She often felt that way when Spirit congratulated them on good work. She was incredibly lucky to be a Silver Dolphin, and having even more magical skills than most Silver Dolphins was a great honour.

You deserve the praise.

Spirit's voice interrupted her thoughts.

Having such great power is a burden and you work hard to manage the extra responsibility.

Thank you.

Antonia was suddenly overcome with shyness – something she hadn't felt in Spirit's presence for a long time!

Antonia looked around, hoping that Bubbles and Dream might be near.

Softly Spirit clicked a laugh. "Bubbles and Dream have gone fishing, and you have to hurry back, Silver Dolphins. Claudia is waiting for you."

Antonia nodded. Claudia had Silver Dolphin powers too, and even though she didn't swim with the dolphins much these days she still communicated with them. With Cai's help Antonia folded the plastic wrapper into a more manageable bundle, then towed it ashore. Spirit watched them go, then splashing his tail in the water swam back out to sea. Antonia

and Cai waded up the beach, laughing together as the water gushed from their clothes.

"I love being a Silver Dolphin," said Cai. "It's the best thing that's ever happened to me."

"Me too." Antonia put the plastic sheet on the sand while she combed the tangles from her damp hair with her fingers and put on her shoes.

At a slower pace she and Cai climbed up the cliff path and picked their way round the nesting puffins. Claudia's empty car was parked on the road, but they soon spotted her walking along the cliffs.

"How did the rescue go?" she asked.

"It was good," said Antonia. "We rescued a puffin tangled in this. We think it came from the building site."

Claudia took the plastic from Antonia and examined it.

"Hmm," she said thoughtfully. "It certainly looks that way. We'll hang on to this for a bit. It might be useful."

Claudia didn't say any more as she led the way back to the car, but Antonia sensed she was thinking the same thing as her. This couldn't go on. It was an enormous task just keeping the puffins away from the road without worrying about rubbish too. Something had to be done about the building site.

Chapter Six

That evening Antonia borrowed her dad's computer to look on the internet for information about puffins. There were lots of websites on the colourful birds and some amazing news reports on pufflings. Early the following morning Antonia waited impatiently for Claudia and Cai to pick her up for puffling patrol. She'd barely done up her seat belt before she was telling them all the things she'd found out.

"The pufflings are like baby turtles," she started. "Remember how we saved the hatchlings in Australia when the hotel lights confused them and they went the wrong way up the beach?"

"Please tell me that pufflings don't do the same thing," groaned Cai.

"They do," said Antonia. "At the end of summer when it's time for the pufflings to leave the nest and fly out to sea they often get confused by artificial lights and go the wrong way. In places like Scandinavia and Alaska towns by the sea have puffin patrols just like us. It's an annual event. People go out at night and rescue the pufflings before

they get run over, or eaten by cats." Antonia shuddered. "I read about it online in local newspapers."

"That won't happen to our pufflings," said Cai. "There aren't any lights at night-time. It's just a building site."

"Not this year," Antonia agreed. "But what about next year? When the apartments are finished there'll be lights."

"I've been thinking about that too," said Claudia, glancing at Antonia in the rear-view mirror. "When people start living here there'll be lots of traffic at all hours of the day."

"So what can we do about it?" asked Cai helplessly.

"The easy solution would be to build a fence along the side of the road," said Claudia. "I've decided to ask for a meeting with the building company to discuss the problems they're causing, firstly with their waste, but also the long-term problems for the birds. I'm going to ask if they can build a permanent fence."

"Can we come with you? Please, Aunty Claudia," begged Cai.

"We're good at persuading people to help us," Antonia joined in.

Claudia smiled. "It's an excellent idea. It might make the builders think about how their actions are affecting everyone's future. I'll make an appointment with them for after school."

"It doesn't *have* to be after school," said Cai cheekily. "In school time is fine by me. Maths is a very good lesson to miss."

"Definitely," Antonia agreed.

Claudia chuckled. "Bad children!" she exclaimed.

There was much more traffic at the building site that morning and Antonia and Cai were kept so busy chasing after the pufflings that they only just made it to school on time.

"What kept you?" asked Sophie, who was waiting impatiently in the playground with Toby.

"Sorry," Antonia apologised, straightening the uniform she had only just pulled on in the car.

"Lauren was asking where you were," said Sophie. "Does this mean you two are getting on at last?"

Antonia shrugged. She couldn't imagine why

Lauren would be looking for her. She certainly hadn't got the impression that they were friends.

"Never mind," said Sophie. "You're here now. And there's the bell, just when I wanted to tell you about my new art project."

Sophie was a keen artist and rarely went anywhere without her sketchbook.

"Tell me as we go in," said Antonia.

Sophie grinned. "Well, you know how I'm good at drawing cats and making jewellery? Dad suggested I combined the two skills and designed my own range of cat jewellery for people to wear."

"It sounds fantastic," said Antonia, genuinely impressed. "Can I come round and see what you've made?"

"There isn't much to see yet," admitted Sophie. "But come round anyway. It's ages since we got together."

When Antonia reached the classroom Becky was perched on her desk watching Lauren count out an enormous stack of coloured envelopes. She giggled and nudged Lauren, who stopped counting and looked up. An unpleasant smile crossed her face.

"Hello, Toni! You're just in time to help me work out a maths problem," Lauren said in a silly sing-song voice. "If there are twenty-eight children in our class and I invite all of them to my party, how many invites would I need?"

Antonia sat down and pretended to read the early-morning work that Mrs Howard had written on the white board.

"Hmm," said Lauren, "Toni doesn't know. Can you help her, Becky?"

"Yes Miss, it's twenty-seven," Becky simpered.

"Well done, Becky. So let's count the invites and see how many we have."

Slowly Lauren counted the multicoloured envelopes, noisily slapping each one down on the desk. Becky joined in, counting with gusto.

"Twenty-three, twenty-four, twenty-five," they chanted.

"Oh…" Lauren stopped counting and held up the last envelope. It was red and decorated with swirly gold gel pen writing. "That makes twenty-six. So someone hasn't been invited to my party. I wonder *who*?"

By now Lauren had the attention of most

of the class. Antonia opened her exercise book and began to write. Her face was a similar shade to Lauren's last envelope and she kept her head low to the desk, hoping no one would notice.

"Thank you, Lauren, I'll take those. Becky, go back to your seat and get on with the work." Mrs Howard had silently entered the room and was walking towards them. She gathered up Lauren's envelopes as she swept past and put them in the drawer of her desk.

"But...! You can't take those. They're my party invites," squawked Lauren.

Mrs Howard silenced Lauren with a look.

"This is my time. You can have your letters back at the end of the day, in your time."

Lauren glared at Antonia and mouthed

something. Antonia sighed, knowing that Lauren would blame her for losing the invites and therefore probably spend the day annoying her on purpose. But Mrs Howard watched Lauren like a hawk, and for once the morning passed without incident. At break time Sophie, Cai and Toby bundled Antonia out of the classroom, forming a tight huddle round her in the playground.

"I'm not going to Lauren's party," said Sophie hotly.

"Me neither," said Cai. "When she gives me an invite I'll refuse to take it."

"And me," said Toby. "I won't go either."

Antonia's eyes stung and there was a lump in her throat. Who cared how horrible Lauren was when she had such brilliant friends!

"Thanks," she said, swallowing back the tears. "But you don't have to do that. I don't mind if you want to go to her party."

"Are you mad?" Cai sounded insulted. "I would rather swim with sharks than go to Lauren's party."

"Me too," nodded Sophie.

"Come on," said Toby, suddenly producing a football. "Forget Lauren. She's not worth it. Let's have a kick around."

Antonia spent the whole of break playing football and really enjoyed it. All her tension fell away and she went back to lessons feeling much more cheerful. As the clock hands ticked closer to three fifteen some of her earlier anxiety returned. Outwardly Lauren was being exceptionally good, but she kept shooting

Antonia nasty looks. Quietly Antonia began to gather her things together so she could be first out when the bell went. She wasn't going to hang around and watch Lauren hand out her invites. But instead of sending the class home together Mrs Howard played a game with them, calling out sums and letting those who put their hand up and gave the right answer go home first. Antonia was one of the first to get a sum right and she hared out of school, waiting for Cai at the gate to avoid seeing Lauren dishing out her invites.

"Are you all right?" asked Cai as they walked to Sea Watch.

"Yes, thanks," said Antonia. It wasn't nice being picked on, but she'd dealt with it and she wasn't going to let Lauren's unpleasant

behaviour spoil the rest of her day. "I can't wait to get to Sea Watch. Do you think Claudia managed to arrange a meeting with the builders?"

"Probably," Cai grinned. "Aunty Claudia's very persuasive when she's passionate about something."

"I know. And that's what the puffins need. Come on, let's run."

With her school bag bumping against her back, Antonia raced Cai to Sea Watch.

Chapter Seven

Claudia had arranged a meeting with the building-site foreman for four o'clock the following day.

"You can both come with me and present photographic evidence that you're going to collect today."

"Photographic evidence?" questioned Cai.

"That's right. I'll lend you my camera when

you go on puffling patrol this afternoon so you can photograph the birds. Be extra careful of the road traffic while you're doing it."

"We will be," promised Antonia.

"It's Friday tomorrow, so can Antonia spend the night?" asked Cai.

"Antonia's always welcome," said Claudia.

"Thanks, that'd be cool," said Antonia. "Then we can go to our surfing class together on Saturday morning."

Claudia drove them to Crane Point and left them with her camera and a warning, "Be careful now. Don't do anything silly."

"As if!" Cai exclaimed. "Don't worry, Aunty Claudia. Nothing's going to happen to us."

The pufflings were growing stronger and it was hard work keeping them off the road. No sooner had Antonia and Cai shepherded one group back then more pufflings would appear, waddling like wind-up toys on their stumpy little legs. They took turns taking photos and keeping an eye out for cars. The builders' car park was almost empty when Antonia experienced a familiar sensation that made her heart beat excitedly.

Spirit needed them. With a final glance around to check the pufflings were safe, Antonia edged towards the path that led down to the beach. Seconds later her silver dolphin charm began to vibrate.

Silver Dolphin, we need you.

Spirit, I hear your call.

Antonia answered his silent call in her head. Her dolphin charm tapped against her neck

as she hurtled down the path. She could hear Cai following behind her, his feet pounding in time with the rhythm of her necklace. At last they reached the beach. Spying a rock near the steps, Antonia put Claudia's camera on top and covered it up with her school sweatshirt. Both Antonia and Cai arranged their shoes and socks around the sweatshirt so that it looked like someone had left a jumble of clothes.

"Hopefully no one will notice it," said Cai as they dashed towards the sea.

"Hardly anyone comes here anyway," Antonia commented.

She splashed through the water, dived into a wave and began to swim. Immediately her legs melded together and Antonia, who never tired of becoming a Silver Dolphin, almost cried out with pleasure. She leapt through the water, her body arching above the waves, sparkling droplets of sea water flying from her like diamonds. Antonia felt like she was flying as the Silver Dolphin magic propelled her along.

Spirit was waiting for them with Star, Bubbles and Dream and he smacked his tail on the water in greeting.

"Thank you for answering my call, Silver Dolphins. It's litter picking again. There's a large amount of it floating towards the shore."

"Yuk," said Cai, noticing the rubbish for the first time.

Litterbugs annoyed Antonia. Why were people so lazy? They wouldn't throw food wrappings and empty cans around in their homes, so why throw them around outside?

"At least it's not builders' rubbish this time." Antonia set to work collecting up the torn carrier bags, plastic drinks bottles and sandwich cartons.

"I wonder how this got here?" she asked, fishing a bedraggled shoe from the water.

"Whoever lost it must be hopping mad," said Cai.

"That's a terrible joke," Antonia groaned.

There was too much rubbish to carry so they carefully wrapped it in the torn carrier bags to tow ashore.

"Thank you, Silver Dolphins," said Spirit. "Now you can play."

"Bubbly!" squeaked Bubbles, who'd been hovering nearby, trying not to get in the way. "Let's play sprat. I'll be it. It's a three waves' head start."

"Wait," said Antonia, laughing. "We need to put the rubbish somewhere safe first."

They swam to the beach and left the rubbish away from the surf so that it wouldn't get washed out to sea. Antonia and Cai raced back to the dolphins. Bubbles counted to three while everyone hid. It was great fun playing sprat. Antonia, Cai and Dream lay together in a kelp bed, scattering in opposite directions when Bubbles found them. He chased Antonia, but she was too fast, darting behind a rock and swimming in the opposite direction before he realised her plan.

At last Cai called the game to a halt. "We'd better go. Aunty Claudia will be here soon to pick us up."

Bubbles dived under the water, disappearing

completely, then surfacing right by the Silver
Dolphins and showering them with salty
water.

"Bubbles!" they shrieked.

Bubbles clicked a laugh and splashed the
water with his fins while Cai flicked water
back at him. They rubbed noses goodbye, then
Antonia and Cai swam back to the deserted
beach. They collected their things and shared
out the rubbish. Cai hung the camera around
his neck for the slow climb back up the cliff
path. Claudia's car was parked by the side of
the road. It was empty. Cai spotted her first,
chasing after two pufflings.

"She's not as good as us," he chuckled.

"We've had a lot more practice," said
Antonia fairly.

They left the rubbish by the side of the car and hurried over to help her.

Once the pufflings realised they were outnumbered they gave up quietly and allowed themselves to be shepherded back to their nests.

"Thank goodness you came when you did," panted Claudia. "I'm not as fast as I used to be."

"You're not so bad for an oldie," Cai teased her.

As they walked back to the car Claudia announced that she would do the Friday morning puffling patrol.

"It's going to be a long day for you both with the meeting after school."

"We can manage!" Antonia and Cai protested.

"I'm sure you can, but tomorrow it's my

turn," said Claudia firmly. "Put the rubbish in the boot. We'll take it home with us."

Antonia had a sudden feeling that Claudia missed being a Silver Dolphin. She hadn't given up completely, and filled in when Antonia and Cai were away from Sandy Bay, but it wasn't the same as always answering the call. Antonia knew only too well how it felt to be left out. Her stomach churned uncomfortably at the thought of Lauren's party. Had Lauren given out some of her invites today? Or would she wait until tomorrow when she could embarrass Antonia by handing them out in one go?

"See you at school," said Cai, when Claudia dropped her back home.

"See you at school," agreed Antonia, wishing she could somehow find an excuse not to go.

Chapter Eight

It was nice walking to school with Sophie the following morning. Antonia had missed their early-morning chats.

"I told Lauren that I wouldn't go to her party," Sophie confided. "So did Cai, Toby, Alicia, Isabel and Rosie. They all thought Lauren was being mean."

Antonia sighed, glad that Lauren had given out some of her invites, but fed up with her nastiness and how she was dividing the class. "I didn't mind not being invited," she said. "But I did mind being not invited so publicly."

"When are you coming round to see my cat jewellery?" asked Sophie.

Antonia shifted her overnight bag into her other hand.

"I'm staying the night at Cai's and then I'm surfing tomorrow morning, but I'd love to come in the afternoon if you're around?"

"Great," said Sophie. "That'll give me a bit longer to make some more pieces. I've had a brilliant idea for a bracelet."

At school Antonia hung her overnight bag on her peg before going into the classroom. Lauren

followed her in and began a loud conversation with Becky about what she was wearing for her party. It was going to be a long day. That morning Mrs Howard set the class a maths challenge, then spent most of her time helping people. Moving around the class, the teacher wasn't aware of Lauren's taunts and the way she kept deliberately knocking Antonia's things from the table. Antonia kept her mouth firmly shut, digging her nails in her palms to stop herself from retorting each time Lauren "accidentally" threw something else to the floor. When the lunchtime bell went Antonia hung back, pretending to be finishing her maths work to avoid a confrontation with Lauren in the cramped cloakroom. When she was the last one in the classroom Antonia handed in her

book and went out to lunch. The cloakroom hadn't cleared. A laughing crowd of her classmates were being entertained by Lauren.

"And here we have the latest fashion in pyjamas." Lauren held up a familiar-looking pair of star-patterned pyjamas. "Not to my taste, but luckily *I* don't have to wear them."

The group laughed as Lauren tossed the pyjamas aside, picking up a fluffy pair of polar bear slippers. "Look at these! Aren't they so last year?"

There was a loud roaring in Antonia's head. Blood rushed to her face, making her cheeks flame with embarrassment and fury. *Those were her things!* How dare Lauren go through her bag!

"Stop!" she bellowed. "Give those back. They're mine."

It was satisfying to see the surprised look on Lauren's face, but Antonia was too angry to dwell on it. Holding out her hand she marched straight up to Lauren.

"Give me back my bag."

"Say please," jeered Lauren, whisking the bag out of Antonia's reach.

"Give me my bag."

Lauren pulled out Antonia's favourite teddy bear and wiggled it in front of her face.

"Mr Bear didn't hear you say please."

Something inside Antonia snapped. White-hot anger coursed through her, making her react without thinking.

"That's because I didn't say it," she shouted. "Why should I say please to someone as silly and mean as you? I can't believe that you've

been allowed to move up to Year Six. My little sister's got more sense than you and she's in Year Three. You're not clever and you're definitely not funny. You're plain sad."

"You're the sad one," said Lauren, tipping Antonia's bag upside-down and strewing the contents around the cloakroom. "I mean, who wears stuff like this?"

"*Enough!* I am ashamed of you, Lauren Hampton." Mrs Howard stepped into the cloakroom and fixed Lauren with her deadliest stare. "Would it be so funny if it was your nightwear being held up for inspection? I think not. Pick up Antonia's things at once, then go and stand outside the staffroom. I will deal with you shortly. And the rest of you, outside now until you are called in for lunch."

The class melted away as a red-faced Lauren retrieved Antonia's things and furiously stuffed them back in her bag.

"I'll do it." Antonia pulled the bag away from Lauren and finished repacking it. Lauren flounced off to wait outside the staffroom and Antonia scanned the floor to check that she hadn't missed anything.

"Antonia…"

Antonia glanced up in surprise. She'd forgotten abut Mrs Howard.

"I'm sorry about that. It won't happen again."

Antonia blushed. "Thanks," she mumbled, then hung up her bag and hurried outside.

Lauren was very quiet that afternoon and completely ignored Antonia. It was a huge

relief when the day ended and Antonia was able to go to Sea Watch with Cai. They arrived out of breath from running. Claudia was pleased to see them.

"The meeting's at four o'clock. Leave your school bags up at the house and get in the car while I tell Sally that we're going out."

She strode off to talk to Sally, an adult volunteer who often looked after Sea Watch when Claudia was elsewhere.

Antonia's stomach fluttered nervously. Could they persuade the builders to be more careful with their rubbish? And would they be prepared to build a fence to keep the pufflings safe? After leaving her bag in the kitchen Antonia climbed into the car with Cai.

"Aunty Claudia, are you going to brush your

hair?" asked Cai hesitantly, when Claudia joined them.

"Pardon? Oh!" Catching sight of herself in the rear-view mirror, Claudia grinned. "I am a bit on the wild side."

Using her hand Claudia smoothed down her unruly curls and rubbed a smudge of dirt from her nose.

"We've been busy today. Someone brought in a stray dog. He was really dirty and full of fleas."

"A dog!" exclaimed Antonia. "Are we taking in pets now as well?"

"No we are not," said Claudia with a laugh. "There simply isn't room. But the lady who brought him in didn't have a car so asked if we could take him over to the local dog shelter. Now when we get to Crane Point remind me

to get the plastic you found yesterday out of the boot and take it into the meeting."

There were pufflings near the road when they arrived at the building site. Claudia stopped the car to let Cai and Antonia get out and herd them back to the cliffs.

"Shall we take more photos?" asked Cai.

"No need," said Claudia. "The ones you took yesterday are brilliant. If the foreman needs more evidence he can come and see for himself."

Antonia was even more nervous as they walked towards the building site. What if the foreman refused to help them? They had managed to protect the pufflings this season, but what about next year and the year after that? Tightly crossing her fingers, she willed the meeting to go well.

Chapter Nine

Claudia collected the plastic packaging and a folder from the boot of her car then led the way on to the building site through a gate in the temporary metal fence. The moment they stepped inside a builder collared them.

"Can I help you?" he asked.

"We've an appointment with Mr Wilson at four o'clock," said Claudia pleasantly.

"Right-io! Wait here please and I'll get you kitted out." The man walked up to a long white trailer, opened the door and disappeared. Several minutes later he reappeared carrying an armful of bright yellow clothing.

"What the…" exclaimed Cai. "I have a bad feeling about this."

"Sssh," said Antonia.

"Health and Safety regulations," said the builder. He handed round bright yellow high-visibility jackets and matching yellow helmets.

"Is the meeting over there then?" asked Cai, pointing at the building works.

"No, but every visitor who comes inside the compound has to be kitted out in the correct safety gear. It's the regulations," explained the man.

Antonia's hat was too big for her and kept slipping over her eyes.

I'd have thought your hat was a bigger danger than the building site.

The voice in Antonia's head was Claudia's. Antonia glanced up and Claudia winked. Antonia grinned back. The building site with its huge, noisy machines was a scary place and she was glad Claudia was there too.

They followed the builder over to the trailer and up the metal steps. The trailer groaned and the floor rocked as they filed inside. It was the same sensation as being on board a boat. The trailer was brightly lit with fluorescent lighting and had a small reception

area where a bored-looking woman was typing at a computer.

"Mr Wilson's visitors," said the builder, leaving them at the desk.

"Sign in, please. You'll need to wear one of these." The lady stopped typing and slid three enormous visitor badges across the desk.

"I'm beginning to feel like a Christmas tree," muttered Cai.

Antonia swallowed a nervous laugh as she pinned the badge on her visibility jacket. The walls of the trailer were thin and they could hear Mr Wilson talking to someone on a telephone. At last it went quiet, then the trailer rocked as he moved to open his door.

"Claudia Neal?" He extended a hand and shook Claudia's vigorously. "Bill Wilson. Good to meet you. "And who do we have here?"

"Cai Pacific," said Cai, boldly offering his own hand.

"Good to meet you, Cai."

"Antonia Lee," said Antonia, shyly shaking hands.

"Come in then, take a seat. Pull up an extra one from over there. Now, how can I help?"

Claudia laid the plastic wrapping on the desk alongside her folder containing the photographs of the puffins and their young. She breathed deeply, then began to talk slowly, clearly and with passion in her voice as she explained the damaging effects that the building site was having on the local environment. There was a deep silence when she'd finished, broken only by the scratch of Mr Wilson's pen as he rapidly

made notes on a lined pad. At last he put his pen down and Antonia, who'd almost forgotten about breathing, exhaled.

"The rubbish is inexcusable," said Mr Wilson, his voice grave. "We have a responsibility to be good neighbours and clearly we are failing that duty. I will speak to my site supervisor. We should not be polluting the area. We can also do something about the puffins. I suggest we run a temporary metal fence alongside the road while the building work is in progress."

"That's fantastic. Thank you," said Claudia, her sea-green eyes crinkling up in delight.

"But what about next year? When you've gone..." The words were out before Antonia could stop them.

"Next year is a little more complicated," said the foreman, carefully choosing his words. "The obvious solution would be to construct a permanent fence, but that would cost money. The economic climate being what it is means that we are constantly looking to reduce our overheads. I'm not sure that our parent building company would be prepared to go to such an expense. Naturally it would affect our unit price, which we are trying to keep to a minimum."

Antonia's head whirled like it did at school when she didn't understand a problem. Whatever did Mr Wilson mean?

"You're saying that a fence is too expensive," stated Claudia.

"Yes." Mr Wilson shifted uncomfortably under Claudia's unwavering stare.

"What if we paid for it?" asked Antonia. She thought about her pocket money, knowing it wouldn't even cover one fence post. But the puffins needed a fence. The puffling patrol had been successful, but it took up so much time. It would be impossible to keep an eye on the birds forever.

"I'd have to ask my bosses. I can't see a problem, but landscaping is important when selling our properties. I'll need to check that a permanent fence would fit with the overall design. It will be expensive. Does your charity have that sort of money?" Mr Wilson asked.

"We could raise it," said Cai determinedly.

"Yes," agreed Antonia. "We'll collect it somehow."

Mr Wilson leant forward in his chair. "Good

for you," he said, smiling. "It's refreshing to see young people taking an interest in their community. Let me know what you plan to do and I'll see if I can get down and support you. And don't worry about your patrol tonight. We'll get that temporary fence up straight away."

There were more handshakes, then Mr Wilson escorted them back to the compound gates where he reclaimed their high-visibility jackets and helmets. As they left the compound Antonia saw Lauren's dad. He stared at her, then, realising where he'd seen her before, grinned nastily and flapped his arms. Antonia felt a sudden pang of sympathy for Lauren. No wonder she was so unpleasant with a father like that!

"I'm glad you're staying the night, Antonia," said Cai, as Claudia drove them back to Sea Watch. "We can start planning how we're going to raise the money for a fence straight away."

Antonia was glad too. There wasn't any time to lose. They had to get a permanent fence in place before the builders moved off site and took their temporary one with them.

Chapter Ten

It was a busy weekend. First thing on Saturday morning Antonia and Cai went up to Crane Point to check on the puffins. True to his word, Mr Wilson had erected a temporary fence alongside the road. Antonia and Cai stood on the verge with their noses pressed to the closely meshed wires and

watched the pufflings waddling around the rocky cliff top.

When they got back they talked about the ideas they'd had to raise money. Cai wanted to hold a sponsored surf competition and Antonia suggested a cake sale. But Claudia thought the best idea was an old-fashioned Bring and Buy sale.

"People bring their unwanted things to sell, and buy things other people don't want," she explained. "It's very easy to set up and usually very popular. You can sell cakes there too."

"Where would we hold it?" asked Cai. "It needs to be somewhere we can attract lots of people. Can we bring our unwanted teachers to sell?"

"Or classmates," joked Antonia. "Actually,

you've just given me an idea. Let's ask Mr Cordier if we can hold our Bring and Buy sale in the playground after school. There's always a ton of parents and grandparents around. We'd make a fortune. Maybe we could set up some games too, like Bash the Rat."

"Is that the one where you put a bean bag down a drainpipe and someone has to try and hit it with a rounders' bat as it slides out? I *love* that game!" cried Cai.

"You could do apple bobbing too, seeing as autumn's on the way," Claudia suggested.

For once Antonia couldn't wait for Monday morning, when they could ask their head teacher if he would let them hold the Bring and Buy sale at school. She rehearsed what she would say during her surfing lesson and

fell off her board three times because she wasn't concentrating. She also told Sophie about it when she visited her on Saturday afternoon. Sophie thought it was a great idea too.

"I've got lots of toys I don't play with any more. You're welcome to those, and I'm sure Mum will make you some cakes for a stall," she said generously.

On Sunday Cai and Antonia talked about making advertising leaflets to hand out at school.

"Parents will love us if they can persuade their kids to clear out their rooms," said Cai.

"Not if they're going to buy someone else's stuff instead," said Antonia. "We'll have to be careful how we word the leaflet and make sure we emphasise the games we're organising too."

Monday morning came at last and Antonia's stomach felt full of dancing butterflies.

"Let's ask Mrs Howard if we can go and see Mr Cordier now," said Antonia as they went into the classroom. "I can't wait until break time."

Mrs Howard was curious about why Antonia and Cai wanted to see the head teacher. When she heard their plans for a Bring and Buy sale she grew very excited.

"This fits in perfectly with the 'Helping Our Community' work," she enthused. "It never occurred to me to do something so practical. Go and see Mr Cordier now and tell him you have my full backing."

To Antonia and Cai's delight Mr Cordier immediately agreed to the sale.

"We'll hold it Friday week. That should give you plenty of time to get organised," he said.

There was a real buzz in the classroom when they reported back and Mrs Howard abandoned her first lesson to talk about the new project. The only person who didn't seem pleased was Lauren.

"It's a good thing the sale isn't *this* Friday," she kept repeating. "Cos that's when my party is."

"That's nice for you," said Antonia pleasantly.

"What?" asked Lauren suspiciously, but Antonia wasn't listening. She had more important things to think about.

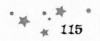

Mr Cordier had said that Antonia and Cai could use the resources room to store things that people brought in to sell.

"Just don't sell any of the school's resources by mistake," he joked.

After school Antonia and Cai walked to Sea Watch. They were planning to spend their time clearing out Cai's bedroom to see if he had anything for the Bring and Buy sale.

"You can help me do my room tomorrow," said Antonia.

But as they turned into Claudia's drive Antonia knew the clear-out would have to wait. Spirit was about to call. Seconds later her silver dolphin charm began to vibrate. She and Cai sprinted down the garden and through the gate to the beach. They dumped their bags

by the Sea Watch boat and pulled off their shoes and socks.

Spirit, I hear your call.

With her charm thrumming against her neck Antonia waded into the sea.

"Brrr," shivered Cai, splashing alongside her. "It feels colder today."

Taking a deep breath, Antonia plunged headfirst into the water. To begin with the water felt freezing, but as her legs melded together, allowing her to swim like a dolphin, she stopped noticing. Keeping pace with each other, Antonia and Cai swam, guided to Spirit by his whistling.

The call was coming from Gull Bay. Antonia and Cai swam side by side as they raced to find him, and a short while later Antonia

spotted five silver heads bobbing up and down together.

"Over there," she whistled, altering her direction. "Spirit and his family, and who's that?"

"I don't know," clicked Cai. "It's a common dolphin… so someone from their pod maybe?"

The new dolphin was the same size as Dream and had silver-grey skin, friendly eyes and a small nick on his dorsal fin.

"Silver Dolphins," clicked Spirit as they approached. "Thank you for answering my call."

"How can we help?" asked Antonia, rubbing his nose in greeting.

Spirit rubbed Cai and Antonia's noses, and Bubbles, Dream, Star and the other dolphin

all smacked their fins on the water by way of hello.

"This is Phantom," said Spirit. "He's Bubbles and Dream's friend. They were messing around on the ocean bed when Phantom grazed his nose on some glass. It's not that bad and it doesn't need healing, but the glass is half buried in the sand and needs removing before it causes another injury."

Antonia was glad that Phantom wasn't hurt, but a little disappointed that she wasn't needed to use her healing magic. She was about to dive down to the seabed when Dream clicked, "We're not allowed to help in case we get injured, but Dad said we can play when you've finished."

"Bubbly!" clicked Antonia. "This shouldn't take long."

She dived down, hair streaming behind her as she made for the seabed. The water was murkier than she'd expected, and reaching the bottom Antonia swam slowly, concentrating on finding the glass. A short distance away Cai swam with his arms outstretched, tracing his fingers along the sand. Several times Antonia saw something glinting and thought she'd found the glass, but each time it turned out to be a pebble or sparkly grain of sand. She found a small broken toy helicopter and put it in the pocket of her school trousers to dispose of in a bin. Then, widening her search area, Antonia swam towards a small cluster of rocks encrusted with barnacles and green seaweed and began searching there.

"Ouch!" cried Cai suddenly.

Antonia swung round. "Are you all right?"

"No, but I think I've found the glass." Cai sucked the palm of his right hand while he carefully dug around in the sand with his left.

"Here, let me." Antonia came to help and Cai gratefully let her take over.

"That was stupid," he muttered. "It really stings."

"I'm not surprised. Look at this." Antonia unearthed two razor-sharp halves of a broken bottle. "Why are people so careless?"

"Hmm," murmured Cai.

"Cai? Are you all right?"

Antonia had been looking around for a suitable piece of seaweed to wrap the broken glass in, when something about Cai's tone made her stop.

"I'm bleeding a bit, that's all."

"Let me see." Antonia wedged the glass on the cluster of rocks and went to look at Cai's hand.

"Right." Antonia forced herself to breathe slowly as she examined the wound, a deep gash crossing Cai's palm from the base of his little finger to the base of his thumb.

"It's not OK, is it?" asked Cai.

"No," said Antonia, unable to lie to her friend. "It's bleeding quite badly. It's going to need stitches."

Chapter Eleven

Although they were still underwater, blood was flowing from the cut and running down Cai's arm.

"Hold your hand up," said Antonia, remembering some of the first-aid training she'd been given in her surfing class. "It'll slow down the bleeding."

Cai raised his hand above his head and the blood continued to trickle down his arm. Antonia tried not to panic. Cai needed to get to hospital fast, but they were so far out to sea that it would take ages to get there.

"Silver Dolphins, what's up?" Spirit appeared as if from nowhere. "I sense trouble."

"Cai's cut himself. He needs stitches," said Antonia. "The glass is over there. Don't touch it. I'll come back for it later."

"Star, Bubbles, Dream, come quickly," whistled Spirit. "They can get you seaweed to make a bandage," he added.

"My arm's aching. Can I put it down?" asked Cai.

He lowered his hand and Antonia reached out for it. The sight of the blood made her

stomach queasy. It was bad enough seeing the sea life hurt, but to see Cai injured was very frightening. The blood was pumping out quite fast. What if the seaweed wasn't enough to stem the flow? Antonia wished she had a mobile phone so she could call for an ambulance. But an ambulance was no good to Cai out here.

I'm useless she thought.

No, you're not.

Spirit's voice calmly sounded in her head.

Think of all the times you have helped us.

Memories of previous rescues flitted through Antonia's mind. Dream had been badly injured once, when she'd been hit by a speedboat, and another time Star had cut her nose on a bottle. Antonia was remembering how she'd helped them when a commotion in the water broke her train of thought. Bubbles, Dream, Star and Phantom swam round her and Cai with anxious eyes.

"What's happened?" they clicked.

"Cai's cut himself. We need seaweed for a bandage," Spirit clicked back.

Immediately the dolphins took off, searching the seaweed-draped rocks for a suitable bandage. Antonia hardly noticed them go. She held on to Cai's bleeding hand, firmly but gently pressing the cut together with her fingers as she tried to stem the bleeding. Suddenly Antonia experienced a warm feeling that spread down her arm. Startled she gripped Cai's hand more firmly, making him squeak.

"Sorry!"

The warmth was developing into a tingling sensation coursing through Antonia's fingers. Her head whirled. What was happening? Surely she couldn't heal people too, could she? As doubt consumed her the tingling began to fade. *No!* Antonia pushed the doubts away and concentrated on the magic. She could do this. She could heal Cai.

Heal.

The word ran through her head as she willed Cai's hand to heal. Antonia imagined his brown skin knitting together, forcing the bleeding to stop. She could feel Cai trembling as she pushed her fingers more firmly down on the wound. Her own fingers were warm and tingling as the magic flowed through them.

Cai stared at her, his eyes round with awe,

until suddenly he pulled his hand away.

"It's better," he gasped. "It was stinging like mad, but it doesn't hurt now."

"Here, let me see." Antonia pulled his hand back and stared at the palm with a mixture of incredulity and pride. The wound had healed completely, with only a faint line in Cai's skin to show for it.

"That was amazing! I never knew you could do that!" Cai couldn't stop staring at Antonia.

"Me neither," she whispered.

Spirit swam over and bowed his head respectfully.

"Silver Dolphin, your special magic grows stronger still. I didn't know someone as young as you could be powerful enough to heal another Silver Dolphin. You have shown me

something I thought impossible. I'm so proud of you."

"Thank you," stammered Antonia.

This new power was a shock to her too. She thought she'd reached the peak of her magical abilities. It was incredible to learn she could do more. But how much more was she capable of? Could she heal anyone in the sea who needed her help, or only another Silver Dolphin?

Only a Silver Dolphin, I'm afraid.

Claudia!

Antonia was delighted to hear her friend's voice in her head.

Silver Dolphins are protectors of the sea, so your magic can protect them when they are answering the call.

Is that how I healed Cai?

Yes, but like Spirit said, it is very rare for someone so young to learn this skill. Yours is a very special talent. Well done, my rising star.

Thank you.

Antonia's face flamed with embarrassment.

"What?" asked Cai. "Why are you blushing?"

"It's nothing," said Antonia.

A mixture of emotions and a large amount of relief made Antonia convulse with laughter as Bubbles and the other dolphins approached. "Look, Cai. Look how much seaweed everyone's collected. There's enough there to bandage a whale."

Cai's recovery was complete. He and Antonia hoped they would still be allowed to

play with Bubbles, Dream and Phantom, but sensible Star wouldn't hear of it.

"You've had a shock," she said firmly. "You must both go home and rest. You can play next time."

"Aw, Mum!" protested Bubbles, but Star fixed him with a steely eye and would not change her mind.

"You can swim the Silver Dolphins back to where they came from," said Spirit. "But no messing around, Bubbles."

"Me, mess around!" clicked Bubbles indignantly.

"Yes, you!" Spirit laughed indulgently. Then, suddenly becoming serious, he rubbed noses with Antonia and Cai.

"Goodbye, Silver Dolphins, and thank you."

Antonia fetched the broken glass from the rocks and carried it home, ignoring Cai's protests to let him help. It was lovely swimming with the dolphins, but strange to see Bubbles behaving himself. Secretly Antonia was grateful. She was exhausted after using such strong magic. As they neared Claudia's beach the dolphins swam away to sea. Antonia and Cai watched them go, their silver bodies arching effortlessly in the sparkling water.

"That was eventful," said Cai. "Thanks for fixing me up. It would have been a real pain trying to organise our Bring and Buy sale with a messed-up hand."

To Antonia's surprise Claudia was waiting for them by the Sea Watch boat and insisted

that both she and Cai rested after their adventure with the broken bottle.

"But we wanted to clear out my bedroom," said Cai.

Claudia refused to budge.

"This is bigger than you realise," she said simply. "Not just Cai getting injured, but Antonia's new power. She needs time to recover, or she might spoil her magic."

There was no arguing with that. Neither Antonia nor Cai would do anything to jeopardise the Silver Dolphins. Claudia drove Antonia home and after tea she had a shower, then went straight to bed. She meant to read for a bit, but didn't even manage a page. Antonia was so tired she fell asleep with the book cradled in her hands.

Chapter Twelve

The week passed quickly. At first people were slow to offer things for the Bring and Buy sale, and Antonia and Cai worried they might not have enough. But by Friday they had so many things they started to worry they might not sell it all.

"And there's still another week before the

sale," said Antonia, eyeing the mountain of jumble crammed into the resources room.

"Do you think we'll make enough money to buy a fence?" asked Cai.

"I don't know. Lots of people have said they'll bake cakes for us. That'll help."

Permanent fences were expensive. Antonia and Cai had looked them up on the internet and worked out that it would cost a huge amount of money to fence the road to the new apartments.

"It's a good start." Antonia tried to sound cheerful as they headed outside for the last few minutes of the lunch break. "We'll hold the sponsored surf if we don't make enough money this time."

Before they made it outside they were met

by a noisy stream of wet children coming along the corridor accompanied by a harassed-looking dinner lady.

"Single file. No pushing," she bellowed.

"Is it raining?" asked Antonia in surprise.

"Duh! What does it look like, stupid?" said Lauren nastily, elbowing past.

Lauren was in a foul mood for the rest of the afternoon. "The rain'd better clear for my party," she moaned. "You'd like that, wouldn't you, Toni? I bet you're hoping it's too wet to use the bouncy slide!"

Antonia had forgotten that it was Lauren's party today and was shocked that Lauren thought she'd be mean enough to wish her bad luck.

"You'll have a great time," she said

generously. "Aren't you having a disco as well?"

"Don't think you're going to get an invite out of me by suddenly being nice," said Lauren sourly.

There was no point explaining to Lauren that she didn't want an invite to her party. Sighing softly, Antonia carried on with her work. Just before home time Mrs Howard suggested that it might be a good idea to organise the things brought in for the Bring and Buy sale and start pricing them.

"The caretaker has kindly agreed to unlock the school tomorrow if anyone would like to come and help," she said.

Antonia never thought she'd willingly volunteer to come back to school on a Saturday, but hers and Cai's were the first hands up. She was grateful for all the help Mrs Howard was giving them, but this was a Sea Watch project and she didn't want her teacher taking over.

"Bang goes our surfing lesson tomorrow," said Cai, as they walked to Sea Watch together. The rain had cleared and the pavements sparkled in the afternoon sun.

"It's for a good cause though," said Antonia, stopping to take off her sweatshirt.

At Sea Watch Claudia had exciting news. "Mr Wilson phoned to say his company will allow a permanent fence and he's personally promised to come to your Bring and Buy sale next week."

"Fantastic," said Cai. "At least we'll have one customer."

"And the other good news is that the deepwater pool is finished. I've just been waiting for all my volunteers to come home from school before I start filling it with water."

"Hooray!" cheered Antonia. "Tilly's going to love it."

"Tilly won't be using it for a few days. Once the pool is filled we have to let the water settle and check that the filtration's working properly."

"Are we filling it with sea water?" asked Cai.

"Fresh water from the outside tap," said Claudia. "Seals and sea birds can manage with fresh water while they're being rehabilitated."

While they were waiting for the rest of the Sea Watch volunteers to arrive, Antonia and

Cai fixed the hose to the outside tap and unravelled it.

"It only just reaches." Cai lowered the end of the hose into the pool and straightened out the kinks.

"It's going to take ages to fill," commented Antonia.

"Not half as long as if we'd had to carry buckets of water from the sea," said Cai.

The outside door in the Sea Watch building opened and a chattering group of volunteers headed across the garden to the new pool. Emily, Eleanor, Karen, Oliver and Eddie crowded round and peered through the meshing.

Claudia joined them a few minutes later and everyone fell silent.

"Emily, would you like the honour of turning on the tap?" Claudia asked.

"Me?" Emily went pink with pleasure.

Antonia hid a smile as Emily stumbled forward. Emily was a keen volunteer and often took on the less pleasant jobs that no one else wanted to do. Her parents had given Sea Watch a large donation that paid for the building of the deepwater pool. Antonia was pleased that Claudia had picked her for such a special role.

"On the count of three," said Claudia, her sea-green eyes sparkling merrily.

"One, two, THREE," the Sea Watch volunteers shouted.

Emily switched on the tap. Nothing happened. The hose began to hiss, then suddenly it writhed like a snake flipping upwards as the water spurted out.

"Ew!" squealed the volunteers, leaping back to avoid a soaking.

"Sorry," choked Emily, tears of laughter running down her face. "Why am I so accident prone?"

Cai grabbed the end of the hose and guided it back into the pool.

"Hooray!" everyone cheered.

Antonia grinned happily. Soon Tilly would have somewhere safe to swim while she grew strong enough to be released back into the wild. She glanced over at the seal, who was snuffling around in her pen. Her thoughts turned to the inquisitive pufflings hopping beside the new fence. They were safe too,

while the builders were still working on the new apartments. But they wouldn't be safe when they left. They had to raise the money to buy a permanent fence. Scrunching her hands into her pockets, Antonia vowed that whatever it took she and Cai would raise that money.

Chapter Thirteen

onday morning Lauren brought to school a pile of photos taken at her party. She handed them round the table, throwing spiteful glances at Antonia.

"It looks like you had a great time," said Antonia lightly.

"We did. Shame you missed it," said Lauren nastily.

Antonia didn't bother to point out that she hadn't exactly *missed* it, or that she'd had a great time herself at Sea Watch.

It was a busy week. Antonia and Cai loaded the pictures they'd taken of the pufflings on to the school computer and used them to make posters to advertise the Bring and Buy sale. They pinned several up in and around school and gave some to Emily. Her parents owned a gift shop in town and knew lots of shop owners who were happy to stick the posters in their windows.

Amid all the things they needed to do Antonia and Cai still made time to go and check on the pufflings, who were growing bigger by the day.

"They look like they'll be ready to fly away soon," commented Cai.

"That's good, because the summer is nearly over. It's much cooler than it was," said Antonia wistfully.

The weather was quickly getting colder. Thursday was chilly and overcast and Friday morning Antonia woke with a feeling of doom. She lay in bed with her eyes tightly shut as she realised why she was feeling so bad. It couldn't be! Leaping out of bed Antonia pulled open her blind, hoping that she was wrong. Rain splattered on her sloping attic window.

"No!" She stared at the rain in disbelief.

This couldn't be happening. How could they hold a Bring and Buy sale in the playground if it was raining? Antonia ran downstairs in her pyjamas and threw open the kitchen door. Her parents looked up in surprise from their steaming mugs of tea.

"Where's the fire?" asked Dad placidly.

"Rain, not fire," said Antonia shortly. "It's going to ruin our Bring and Buy sale."

"The sale isn't until this afternoon," said Mum encouragingly. "It'll probably have cleared by then."

"But what if it hasn't?"

"You'll have to postpone it."

"We *can't,*" said Antonia. "Everyone's worked so hard. And Mr Cordier's been really nice about us taking over the resources room. What if he

wants it back and we have to move all the stuff out? There's nowhere else to store it."

"Worrying about it isn't going to help." Mum got up and refilled the kettle. "Go and get dressed while I make you some breakfast."

Slowly Antonia went upstairs. Why couldn't her parents see what a disaster the rain was? They had to have the sale today. They needed to raise the money quickly so there was a permanent fence in place before the builders moved off site taking their temporary fence with them.

Antonia's silver dolphin charm fluttered against her neck. She froze, wondering why she hadn't sensed that Spirit was about to call. The charm fluttered again. Antonia clasped it lightly between her fingers. It felt

silky-soft to touch, just like Bubbles and Dream.

Have courage, Silver Dolphin.

Antonia started as Spirit's voice rang through her head. Her charm quivered and Antonia clasped it more tightly. Suddenly she felt reassured. She was a Silver Dolphin. She wasn't going to let a bit of rain spoil things. Whatever the weather, she and Cai would find a way of making the Bring and Buy sale happen.

Thank you, she answered.

At school Lauren was crowing. "Brilliant weather, Toni," she said, sniggering. "You're gonna have so much fun selling all that junk in the rain. It's a shame I'm gonna miss it, but Becky and I have got more important

things to do than waste our time getting wet for a bunch of stupid birds, haven't we, Becks?"

"We're going to the cinema," said Becky maliciously. "Who wants to come with us?"

Antonia tried not to look fazed as Becky opened her invite to the class. They could manage with a few less helpers at the sale, but it would be disastrous if everyone dropped out. Luckily Mrs Howard arrived, putting an end to the conversation.

"Good morning, everyone," she said briskly. "Now I know the weather doesn't look good, but it's still only morning so we're not going to worry about it right now. We've got lots of things to organise, so let's get started."

Toby put up his hand.

"We ought to have a back-up plan," he

insisted. "Can we use the hall if it's still raining after school?"

It was a brilliant suggestion. Antonia shot Toby a grateful look.

"Unfortunately the hall's booked out to the After School Club," said Mrs Howard. "They're having some work done on their hut."

Antonia groaned. Wasn't that just typical? The After School Club always met in an old hut on the edge of the playground. Trust them to need the hall today!

"What about those tent things we use for sports day?" said Sophie suddenly. "We could put those up to keep the stalls dry."

"You mean the gazebos," said Mrs Howard.

Antonia's heart soared. What brilliant friends she had! They knew how important

this Bring and Buy sale was to her and Cai. The school had several gazebos they used for the children to shelter from the sun during sports day. Mrs Howard thought it a clever idea too and sent Sophie and Antonia to ask Mr Cordier if they could borrow them.

"You can," he agreed, "but it might be better to postpone the sale if it keeps raining. I can't see many people wanting to come along."

Gloomily Antonia returned to class. Mr Cordier was right. Who would want to come to a Bring and Buy sale in the pouring rain?

By lunchtime things weren't looking too good. Lauren continued to tease Antonia about the weather. Antonia knew from past experience that it was best to ignore Lauren's taunts, but it took enormous self-control not to get upset.

At the beginning of afternoon lessons Mrs Howard asked the class to vote on whether or not they wanted to go through with the sale or postpone it for a drier day. Antonia held her breath as the class voted, knowing that Lauren had persuaded several people to join her and Becky at the cinema. Lots of hands went up to vote for postponing the sale.

"Fourteen," said Mrs Howard, counting them twice to make sure she'd not made a mistake. "Hands up those for holding the sale today."

The remaining fourteen hands went up and Mrs Howard pulled a face.

"A tiebreak. That means I shall have the deciding vote." She paused for a moment, letting her gaze wander round the class.

Antonia silently willed her to say yes. Even if they only raised a small amount of money it would be something. They had to start fundraising before they ran out of time to help the pufflings. Mrs Howard's gaze rested on Cai and then Antonia.

"I'm going to say yes, we go ahead," she said at last.

"Thanks, Mrs Howard," Antonia breathed out in relief. "When can we put up the gazebos?"

Mrs Howard walked across to the window.

"Give it half an hour," she said. "There's a patch of blue in the sky that looks like it might be coming our way."

Chapter Fourteen

Mrs Howard was right. Half an hour later the rain stopped and the sky brightened. The class trooped out into the playground to erect the gazebos. Mr Cordier helped and he was so funny, joking with Mrs Howard and the rest of the class, that the event soon took on a party atmosphere. The sun grew stronger,

making the puddles glisten with tiny rainbows as they dried. Antonia and Cai worked hard, carrying tables out on to the playground and organising groups of children to bring out the jumble and set up the games.

"Float!" exclaimed Mrs Howard. "Who wants to go to the office to get the float?"

Everyone wanted that job because Mrs Howard had told them that the float was the money shopkeepers put in their tills at the beginning of the day so they would have change.

"It's quite warm," said Antonia, hopefully staring at the pale blue sky as she pushed up the sleeves of her sweatshirt.

"It's going to be fine," said Cai.

It was better than fine. The afternoon got

drier and warmer and by three o'clock a large crowd of adults had gathered at the school gates. Mr Cordier let them in early and they hurried across the playground towards the bulging stalls. The cakes went first; Antonia and Sophie were manning the stall and they were amazed at the queue of people waiting to buy. Toys and second-hand books were the next most popular stalls, along with Bash the Rat, run by Toby and Cai. Antonia laughed when Jessica rushed up to her and excitedly squeezed round the back of the stall to say, "Look what I just bought, your old animal hospital set."

"I'd have given it to you if you'd asked," said Antonia, feeling guilty.

"I wouldn't have taken it," said Jessica loftily.

"I wanted to buy it to help raise money for the puffins."

"Thanks, Jess," said Antonia. "I hope you enjoy playing with it."

"I will if you'll play with me. Can we play when you get home?"

"I'm not coming home tonight. I'm sleeping over at Cai's again, but I'll play with you tomorrow."

"Then I'm going to ask if Naomi can come round," said Jessica, hurrying off to the school office to find Mrs Lee.

Antonia needn't have worried about not selling everything. It didn't take long for the tables to empty and by the time the last shopper had left the playground there were only a handful of things left.

Antonia began piling the leftovers into a cardboard box.

"How much do you think we made, only—"

"Look," Cai interrupted her. "That's Mr Wilson coming across the playground with Mr Cordier, Mrs Howard and Aunty Claudia."

"Oh! I'd forgotten he was coming. He's a bit late. There's hardly anything left."

Mr Wilson waved as he approached.

"Just in time," he boomed, pulling out his wallet. "How much for that box of bits?"

"Erm," Antonia hesitated.

"Will this cover it?" Mr Wilson held out a large note.

"Definitely," said Antonia, smiling broadly. "Here, it's all yours."

"So, do you think you raised enough for a fence?"

"Not quite," said Antonia truthfully.

"We're planning more events," added Cai.

Mr Wilson's eyes twinkled.

"No need," he said. "I called my bosses and they were very impressed by the things you do at Sea Watch. They were sure you'd raise lots of money, but thought it might not be enough for a fence. They'd like to help out by giving you the rest of the money needed."

"Really?" Antonia and Cai couldn't stop smiling. "Thanks, Mr Wilson. That's fantastic."

"It's a very generous offer," said Claudia.

Mrs Howard looked like she'd won the lottery.

"This has been our most successful Helping

Our Community work to date," she said joyfully. "Well done, everyone. Cai and Antonia, please take all the money to the office and count it. Mrs Lee will check it for you when you've finished. There's enough helpers here to finish clearing up."

Feeling like she was walking on air, Antonia carried the pots of money into the school building.

"What a brilliant end to the summer," said Cai.

"Totally perfect," said Antonia, although a funny feeling told her that things weren't quite over yet.

Chapter Fifteen

That evening Claudia cooked an enormous pot of spaghetti bolognaise and made a huge jug of her legendary fruit punch. They ate outside, soaking up the last remnants of sunshine until the light began to fade and bats flitted overhead.

"We should go in," said Claudia, not making an effort to move.

Antonia sat up, aware of a familiar feeling washing over her. Spirit was going to call. But what could he want so late at night? She glanced at Claudia and saw her friend watching her intently. Antonia raised her eyebrows, knowing that Claudia had sensed the call too. Pushing back her chair, Antonia stood up at the exact moment her silver dolphin charm began to thrum against her neck.

Silver Dolphin, come quickly.

Spirit, I hear your call.

Seconds later Cai was on his feet murmuring, "Spirit, I hear your call."

"Be careful going though the garden. I'll bring a torch down so you can see where you're going when you get back," Claudia called after them as they sprinted for the beach.

Spirit's call felt urgent. Antonia hoped that the dolphins were all safe as she ran through the gate on to the beach. The tide was out, and leaving their shoes in the Sea Watch boat they ran down the gently sloping expanse of sand to the sea. The water seemed to call to them, and without stopping they waded out until it was deep enough to swim. Excitement coursed through Antonia's body as her legs melded together. Using her special skills to help guide her in the half light she swam towards Spirit. Soon Antonia realised they

were being called eastward towards Crane Point. Immediately she thought of the pufflings. Where they in danger? Sensing vibrations in the water, Antonia swam faster until at last she saw four heads bobbing in the inky-black sea. It was Spirit and his family.

"Silver Dolphins," clicked Spirit. "Thank you for answering my call. There's trouble on the cliffs. A puffling has been injured on some litter. He urgently needs your help."

At once Antonia and Cai swam to the beach. The light was quickly fading as they ran up the cliff path. Their footsteps rang out in the dusky dark and Antonia slowed, hoping they wouldn't frighten the puffins as they burst on to the cliff top. There was a lot of activity. The colourful puffins and their black and white

chicks were milling around, mewling excitedly. Antonia vaguely wondered what all the fuss was about, but there was no time to investigate. Scanning the crowd she looked for a bird in distress.

"Over there," called Cai, "by the cliff edge."

A small puffling was teetering around, frantically trying to break free from a plastic container wedged on his webbed foot. As Antonia and Cai approached, the bird panicked and stumbled backwards.

"Steady," crooned Antonia softly.

Knowing it was dangerous to stand too near the edge of a cliff, Antonia lay on the ground. Cai dropped down beside her and slowly they wiggled closer to the puffling. The bird watched them warily, but he didn't move away.

Antonia reached out and closed her hands round his soft body. At first he wriggled in an attempt to shake her off, but Antonia held him firmly.

"Steady, boy, we're here to help."

Gradually the bird relaxed, although he was still trembling.

"See if you can free him," Antonia whispered to Cai.

Reaching out, Cai pulled the container. It was tightly wedged, but Cai gently twisted it until finally it came free.

"Thanks." Antonia examined the bird's leg, but apart from a small scratch it seemed fine. Releasing the puffling, she slowly wriggled away. The puffling watched her for a second, then suddenly it ran towards the cliff.

"No!" gasped Antonia, hoping she hadn't frightened it.

The puffling began flapping its wings quickly until suddenly it became airborne and with a satisfied squawk flew out to sea. It was like a signal. At once the whole of the cliff top seemed to move. Antonia and Cai stared in amazement at the black tide of puffins and pufflings waddling towards the cliff edge.

"It's time!" cried Cai excitedly. "The birds are migrating for winter."

Wordlessly Antonia and Cai stood up and ran for the cliff path. They hurtled down it almost faster than was safe in the twilight until at last they made it on to the beach.

"Quick," said Antonia, running across the sand and throwing herself into the water.

The dolphins were waiting out at sea. Antonia and Cai swam towards them as the first wave of puffins flew overhead. The air was filled with the soft whooshing of wings. Antonia stared into the dusky night sky. In a fluttering cloud of black more pufflings and their parents launched themselves from the cliffs, flying out to sea. Antonia's tail-like legs tingled with the exertion of keeping her afloat and her neck ached, but her eyes never left the sky as more and more puffins flew away. It was a long time before the sky cleared, leaving only the stragglers. Finally they went too, leaving behind the first stars of the evening twinkling in celebration. Antonia turned to Cai and the dolphins, her eyes shining with excitement.

"That was wonderful," she sighed.

Nature is wonderful.

Claudia's voice was strong and clear in her head.

So is being a Silver Dolphin, Antonia answered back. She was bursting with happiness and aware how privileged she was to be trusted with such a special role. Turning to Spirit she whispered, "Thank you for calling us."

"Thank you for answering our call," clicked Spirit.

Antonia smiled. Answering the call of the dolphins was as natural as breathing. She had to do it! But now it was time to go. Guided by the light of the stars and their dolphin friends, Antonia and Cai swam home.